Kindergarten - Christmas - 1986

Grandma and Grandpa Smith

By Edith Kunhardt
Illustrated by Terri Super

D1543745

A Golden Book • New York
Western Publishing Company, Inc., Racine, Wisconsin 53404

from - Mrs. Kennedy

SAM AND SALLY SMITH lived in the city. They lived with their parents in a tall apartment building. They each had their own room.

Every summer Sam and Sally went to visit their
grandparents in the country. It was their special treat.

Grandma and Grandpa Smith met them at the bus stop.
How happy they were to see Sam and Sally!

"We brought Rex with us so you could see him right away," Grandpa told Sam. Sam ran to the car. Rex licked him all over his face.

Grandma and Sally walked slowly to the car. "Did you get a window seat in the bus?" asked Grandma.

"I had the front seat in the bus," said Sally at almost the same time.

Grandma and Sally laughed and held hands.

At Grandma and Grandpa Smith's house Sam and Sally shared a room. They liked that. They could whisper, and they could stay up later than they did at home.

Grandma and Grandpa wanted to hear all about Mom
and Dad. Dad was their little boy all grown up.

Mom and Dad worked all day. It was nice to be with
Grandma and Grandpa, who were home all day.

Every day of the vacation was busy. Sam and Sally
helped in Grandma's garden. They pulled up weeds. They
raked. Grandma let Sally cut some roses for the dinner
table. Sally was careful not to get pricked by the thorns.

Sally and Sam were helping to build a new birdhouse in Grandpa's shop. "Grandma is growing some beautiful big sunflowers," said Grandpa. "I'll dry the seeds and use them to feed the birds next winter."

Sometimes they all drove to the shopping mall. There were rides outside the stores. Sam and Sally went on the merry-go-round. Then they had ice cream cones.

At the mall Grandma got some new pots and seedlings. "You can help me transplant the seedlings when they get big enough," she said to Sam and Sally.

Grandpa went to the hardware center. He liked to look at all the tools and supplies. He bought a new steel tape measure.

One day Sam and Sally helped Grandma carry some things to the attic. Grandma started looking in a box.

"Oh, look, Sam!" she exclaimed. "Here's something for you to take home. It's your father's old baseball glove. He oiled that glove every night, so it was soft and shiny. And now look at it—it's stiff and dusty."

"And here's an old locket of mine, Sally! Would you like to polish it up and take it home? It has a picture of me when I was little."

Sally and Grandma took the locket downstairs. They used an old toothbrush to scrub the outside of it.

Sally looked and looked at the picture inside the locket. The picture was of a long-haired girl in a high-necked dress.

Then Sally put on the locket. She didn't take it off again the whole time she was there—except when she took baths.

Sam ran outside to find Grandpa.

"Yes, that's your dad's glove all right," Grandpa said. "Let's clean it up so we can have a game of catch. Then you'll see how good the pocket is."

So Sam got some neat's-foot oil and made the glove all soft again. Then he and Grandpa had a game of catch.

On Sam and Sally's last night of vacation,
Grandma and Grandpa took them to a drive-in
movie. They all shared a big bucket of popcorn.
Sam and Sally fell asleep in the car on the way home.

The birdhouse was finished. The next morning, Sam and Sally and Grandma and Grandpa all helped put it up. "We'll think of you every time we feed the birds this winter," said Grandma.

Then it was time for Sam and Sally to go home.

Sally took some fresh flowers for Mom. They were wrapped up in wet newspaper, so they wouldn't wilt. Sam carried the baseball glove.

"Good-by, good-by!" they called, waving. "See you next year!"